leapfrog

Mary and the Fairy

First published in 2000
Franklin Watts
96 Leonard Street
London
EC2A 4XD

Franklin Watts Australia
45-51 Huntley Street
Alexandria
NSW 2015

Text © Penny Dolan 2000
Illustration © Deborah Allwright 2000

A CIP catalogue record for this book is available
from the British Library.

ISBN 0 7496 3927 X (hbk)
ISBN 0 7496 4633 0 (pbk)

Series Editor: Louise John
Series Advisor: Dr Barrie Wade
Series Designer: Jason Anscomb

Printed in China

Mary and the Fairy

by Penny Dolan

Illustrated by Deborah Allwright

W
FRANKLIN WATTS
LONDON•SYDNEY

A fairy flew in through Mary's window.

"Mary, why are you so sad?" she asked.

"I've got nothing to wear to the party," Mary said.

The fairy smiled.

"Mary, you *shall* go to the Ball!" she cried.

"Wait ..." stammered Mary.

But the fairy wasn't
listening at all.

"How about a red frock?" asked the fairy.

The red frock made
Mary feel terribly hot.
"But ..." she said.

"Well, what about a blue frock?" asked the fairy.

The blue frock made
Mary feel terribly glum.
"No!" she said.

"I know! A yellow frock!"
the fairy cried.

The yellow frock made Mary's eyes go terribly wiggly.

"I've got it this time! A green frock!" shouted the fairy.

The green frock made Mary's
tummy feel terribly wobbly.
"Yuk!" she said.

"No, don't tell me ... you want a white frock!" guessed the fairy.

The white frock made
Mary feel terribly shivery.
"Stop!" shouted Mary.

"What colour frock *do* you want?" said the fairy crossly.

"I haven't got all day, you know!"

"I don't want a frock," Mary sighed.

"What I really want, is ..."

"Oh, I see!" said the fairy.

She waved her wand again.

"Is that right?" she asked.

"Oh, yes! Thank you, fairy," cried Mary.

"Now, I shall go to the fancy dress party."

Leapfrog has been specially designed to fit the requirements of the National Literacy Strategy. It offers real books for beginning readers by top authors and illustrators.

There are 25 Leapfrog stories to choose from:

The Bossy Cockerel
Written by Margaret Nash,
illustrated by Elisabeth Moseng

Bill's Baggy Trousers
Written by Susan Gates,
illustrated by Anni Axworthy

Mr Spotty's Potty
Written by Hilary Robinson,
illustrated by Peter Utton

Little Joe's Big Race
Written by Andy Blackford,
illustrated by Tim Archbold

The Little Star
Written by Deborah Nash,
illustrated by Richard Morgan

The Cheeky Monkey
Written by Anne Cassidy,
illustrated by Lisa Smith

Selfish Sophie
Written by Damian Kelleher,
illustrated by Georgie Birkett

Recycled!
Written by Jillian Powell,
illustrated by Amanda Wood

Felix on the Move
Written by Maeve Friel,
illustrated by Beccy Blake

Pippa and Poppa
Written by Anne Cassidy,
illustrated by Philip Norman

Jack's Party
Written by Ann Bryant,
illustrated by Claire Henley

The Best Snowman
Written by Margaret Nash,
illustrated by Jörg Saupe

Eight Enormous Elephants
Written by Penny Dolan,
illustrated by Leo Broadley

Mary and the Fairy
Written by Penny Dolan,
illustrated by Deborah Allwright

The Crying Princess
Written by Anne Cassidy,
illustrated by Colin Paine

Cinderella
Written by Barrie Wade,
illustrated by Julie Monks

The Three Little Pigs
Written by Maggie Moore,
illustrated by Rob Hefferan

The Three Billy Goats Gruff
Written by Barrie Wade,
illustrated by Nicola Evans

Goldilocks and the Three Bears
Written by Barrie Wade,
illustrated by Kristina Stephenson

Jack and the Beanstalk
Written by Maggie Moore,
illustrated by Steve Cox

Little Red Riding Hood
Written by Maggie Moore,
illustrated by Paula Knight

Jasper and Jess
Written by Anne Cassidy,
illustrated by François Hal

The Lazy Scarecrow
Written by Jillian Powell,
illustrated by Jayne Coughlin

The Naughty Puppy
Written by Jillian Powell,
illustrated by Summer Durantz

Freddie's Fears
Written by Hilary Robinson,
illustrated by Ross Collins